ORGAN MUSIC

ORGAN MUSIC

MARGARET MAHY

GECKO PRESS

First published in 2010 by Gecko Press
PO Box 9335, Marion Square, Wellington 6141, New Zealand
info@geckopress.com

Text © 2010 Margaret Mahy

 Gecko Press acknowledges the generous
support of Creative New Zealand.

National Library of New Zealand Cataloguing-in-Publication Data

Mahy, Margaret.
Organ music / Margaret Mahy.
ISBN 978-1-87746-747-9
[1. Genetic engineering—Fiction. 2. Bioethics—Fiction. 3. Science fiction.] I. Title.
NZ823.2—dc 22

Cover illustration © 2010 Gavin Bishop
Design by Spencer Levine, Wellington, New Zealand
Printed by Everbest, China

For more curiously good books, visit www.geckopress.com

1

'Look!' said Harley.

'What?' said David.

They had come to a standstill under a streetlight between the smudgy brick walls and broken windows of Forbes Street. An upstairs window suddenly shone out like a jagged star of dirty gold. Looking up at the stab of light, David saw the bricks below it were striped with graffiti. The same few words were scrawled on top of one another, but in different colours. *Where's Quinta?* someone was asking, over and over again. The senseless question staggered from wall to wall.

It was Harley's fault they were picking their way through such a dangerous part of town.

'It'll be cool,' Harley had said. 'Forbes Street's really wild. Glue sniffers are scared to go there. Even the police are.'

But Forbes Street was not wild – just poor and dirty. It was people who made a city dangerous, and Forbes Street was deserted. Yet there must have been someone around somewhere, because Harley, standing under a street lamp, was staring at a car – an ordinary, battered, smeary, blue car.

'Might belong to a drug dealer.' David's voice was sarcastic.

'No! Look! *There!*' Harley hissed. 'They've left the keys in it.'

Sure enough, dangling from the ignition was a round silver ball on a silver chain. It seemed to wink at David.

'Twinkledandory!' said David.

'Stop it,' said Harley. 'You sound such a nerd.'

'I like words,' said David. 'I like inventing them.'

'Well I don't,' Harley said. 'Skip it. Look at the keys!'

Over the last six months – ever since his mother, the school music teacher, had run away with a jazz guitarist – Harley was more and more intent on living dangerously. The trouble was that he wanted David to come along for the ride.

'Forget it!' said David, staring at the swinging silver ball. It winked at him.

'Why not?' Harley persisted. 'Whoever owns this car is so stupid he deserves to lose it. It would be good for him; he'd take more care of it next time. After we'd had a turn with it, that is.'

'Forget it!' David said. 'Anyway, who'd drive?'

'Well, you wouldn't have to,' Harley said scornfully. 'I would. I'll bet I could drive this thing, and the crate it came in.'

'Yeah, but any cop who sees us will know we're only kids,' said David, immediately irritated with himself for sounding so cautious – so dull. Though he knew so many fierce words, somehow he was always cautious when it came to actual adventures. But no way would he say that he wanted to go straight home – that his mother would already be worrying. Harley, with his hair sticking up like the crest of an excited cockatoo, was ready for anything – reckless and free.

'My uncle showed me how to drive,' said Harley. 'He said that I could drive better than most of the guys he knows.'

'You could be the best driver in the world,' said David. 'But some cop'd still stop us. You're only fourteen and you look about eleven. Not 'cause you're short. It's the way your hair sticks up and your ears stick out. You're an earocomic!'

'Yeah, sure,' mumbled Harley, trying to flatten first his hair and then his ears. He hated being reminded that he was small. 'If we're cruising along, not breaking any rules, no cop'll even look at us.'

He ran around to grab the handle on the driver's side. The door opened so obediently that it frightened David all over again. Things just weren't as easy as that in real life – or they shouldn't be.

'See?' said Harley, sliding sideways into the driver's seat.

'Stupidodorous!' muttered David, but he couldn't

help following. So what if they did get into the car for a minute or two? They could always get out again.

'Wow!' Harley was squinting at the shelf below the instrument panel. 'CDs. Great!'

Then he put his hand on the key. The silver ball on the end of the chain swung slightly, seeming to glance from one to the other of them.

'It's *watching* us,' exclaimed David. 'Autovisulati! Come on, Harl! Let's go or we'll be in big trouble.'

'Got to get home to Mummy, do you?' said Harley. 'Is it getting too late for you? Scared the spooks'll come out?' He flicked at the key chain with a fingernail. 'You just do that word-thing to try to make out you're brave.'

Harley was always accusing David of being frightened of something – of teachers, parents and ghosts.

Harley twisted the key. The car started up, running so smoothly that David had to listen hard to be sure it really was ticking over.

Harley released the handbrake. The car slid forward. David sat back and said nothing. What they were doing was beyond word invention. Harley changed gear.

5

They were really moving now, gliding faster all the time between dingy brick walls. The words *Quinta! Come home!* flashed past, sprayed on the bricks in luminous green paint. But David barely noticed. He and Harley were stealing a car. Actually stealing it. They were involved in vehicularrobberation. From here on in, they were men on the run.

'Let's have some music.' Harley's hands were clenched on the steering wheel.

David squinted at the panel in front of him. One of the buttons said CD, and he pressed it.

'You've got to shove a CD in first,' Harley cried, but music was already pouring in from every direction. Some rock band was really letting go – guitars, amplifiers, keyboards, drums ...

'Cool!' yelled Harley, as David strained to make out the words.

Dilly, *dilly*! Dilly, *dilly! Come and be killed*

> *For you must be stuffed*
> *And my customers be filled.*

David's finger shot out to hit the stop button.

'What did you do that for?' asked Harley crossly.

'Didn't you hear what they were singing?' David asked.

'Nah,' said Harley. 'Good beat, though. Put it on again.'

As the music played they had been sliding smoothly through decaying streets. Now they were out on a well-maintained one-way system – familiar territory.

'Don't speed, or they'll pick us up,' David said.

'I'm not speeding,' Harley snapped, but somehow he sounded less sure of himself. He certainly looked small in the driver's seat; he could barely see over the steering wheel. 'What was so mind-blowing about the words, anyhow?'

'They were about death,' David said.

'Is that all?' Harley said. 'Anyone'd think you were scared of dying. Dilly, dilly dill-head!' His left hand shot out to jab the CD button. 'Let's have that one again.'

Music filled the car once more, but this time the voices were ethereal, the pure voices of some wonderful choir. Yet the words of the song were the same – or almost.

> *Dilly*, dilly! *Dilly*, dilly! *Come and be killed*
> *For you must be unstuffed*
> *So that my customers are filled.*

'Great counter-tenor!' Harley said in a suddenly gentle, appreciative voice, reminding David that Harley, rather unexpectedly, enjoyed classical music. In more normal tones, he added, 'Freaky words!'

'Too freaky,' said David. 'And they've changed a bit, since the last version. Stop the car. I want to get *out*.'

Harley clucked like a chicken.

'Okay! So I'm chicken!' said David. 'Just stop.'

He noted the confident press of Harley's foot towards the floor. There was a pause, followed by anxious shuffling.

'What's wrong?' David asked sharply.

'Nothing,' Harley replied, his voice suddenly high and tight. 'No worries! Just that, well, since you're a mate of mine, I'll run you home.'

'First turn left,' said David.

But Harley drove straight past that turn, and the next.

'What's wrong?' David cried.

'Nothing,' Harley replied again, but his lips were curled back in a wince of fear.

Ahead of them traffic lights turned red. Harley neither stopped nor slowed down. They sped through against the red, and a car, shooting towards them from the right, gave such a blast on its horn that David's head rang with the sound.

'You're mad,' he yelled at Harley. 'Stop! Stop now!'

Harley turned his head and stared at him, panting a little.

'Watch the road! Watch the road!' screamed David.

'I don't have to,' Harley replied in a strangled voice. Slumping back in his seat, he took his foot off the accelerator and held his hands away from the wheel. The soft hum of the car's motor did not decrease. The car did not lose speed. If anything, it seemed to accelerate.

'It's driving itself,' Harley said.

3

Directly ahead of them a glowing ribbon tied in one edge of the city. The motorway! The car seemed to surge forward as if it were eager to show them what it could really do on an open road. It selected the inner lane, and away it went. The hum of its engine deepened into a whispering roar.

'Man!' shrieked Harley. 'What sort of car is this?'

'I told you to leave it alone,' David screamed back.

'You got into it, though, didn't you? It's not all my fault.' Then he wailed, 'It's taking us somewhere. But where?'

'I reckon it's some – some police thing,' David said. 'A trap of some kind. Ultraofficialata!'

'Stop doing that!' yelled Harley. 'It isn't funny.'

David stared wildly out at the motorway flickering past them. They were being swept away from the city. Strange and bleak under its great night lights, the motorway was unrolling out into the country. In the artificial light the trees planted beside it looked artificial too, alien structures put there to fool gullible travellers. The car sped on.

'Willesden Forest,' David read on a great sign that came rushing towards them. 'Turn-off 200 metres.'

The car shifted into the lane for the turn-off.

'Willesden Forest,' yelled Harley. 'That's just *trees*, isn't it?'

'It's a government forest,' David said, trying desperately to work out what might be happening. 'They started a programme on genetically altered trees – special, quick-growing ones.' He remembered something. 'It's run by the forestry department – well, it *used* to be. But the government has a private scientific company running it for them – some big international conglomerate sort of business … '

'I don't care who runs it,' Harley yelled. 'I just want to go home. If I get home,' he bargained with the night air – maybe with the car itself – 'I'll keep out of trouble for the rest of my life.'

As he spoke, they swung off the motorway onto a long, straight road, sealed and fenced on both sides. In front of them, black hills pushed up towards the sky, blotting out the starlight. Willesden Forest came rushing towards them. Somehow it felt as ancient as a forest in a fairy tale, even though the trees had been planted less than twenty-five years ago. At the speed they were travelling it seemed to David that the forest was leaping forward to swallow them alive.

Willesden Forest began with row after row of pines lined up like a *corps de ballet*. Each tree had its lower branches trimmed away so that it stood poised on one grey leg, a spiky green tutu fanning out around it. Some of the blocks were signposted: EXPERIMENTAL BLOCK A 46 one block declared itself as they slid past.

'I feel sick,' moaned Harley. David felt sorry for him, knowing as he did that Harley's toughness had always been faked. Deep down, the world frightened him. And then David thought how completely terrified he was himself, though his terror was different. He was used to being alarmed by life and everyone knew it. That was why Harley teased him.

On and on! The car sped down that straight road which must have been at least three kilometres long. The line of hills showed now and then between the trees, coming closer and closer, until at last one hill thrust out a great black elbow, nudging a crooked curve into the road. They took this curve at such speed that the whole forest seemed to tilt around them, then they swept up and over a rise, only to find themselves looking down on a glowing village – long, low buildings and streets as straight as if they had been ruled, with one building rising above the rest like a cylinder of silver. This whole built-up area was caged in by tall fences of wire mesh and steel pipes, and the road directly ahead was blocked by huge gates.

WILLESDEN EXPERIMENTAL STATION said a notice on the gates. David felt for a second or two that the car was standing still while the words rushed towards them.

'We're going to crash,' screamed Harley, hurling himself sideways, arms clasped over his head.

But the gates – like gates in a fairy tale – swept open, and the car, without the slightest reduction of speed, shot into the complex beyond. It turned left, then right, passing blank windows and doors.

'It's going to be all right,' David said to Harley. 'The car's probably programmed to come back home to the people who ... who invented it. I mean, we'll probably get in trouble, but nothing worse than that. Nothing ...' And here he stopped, surprised at finding himself flooded by a huge relief. Just for a second or two back there he had believed he was being swept to his death. Being in trouble was nothing compared to dying.

The car slowed a little. It turned to the right. Directly in front of them was yet another steel fence, a compound contained within the main compound, and behind this second, smaller fence rose that huge, silver-white cylinder of a building they had seen earlier. It looked like a blunt spaceship, pinned to background darkness by narrow shafts of light.

Something moved. The gate to the cylindrical building was guarded. A man had suddenly appeared and was watching them as the car rolled towards him.

David felt huge relief at seeing another human being in this zone of geometric buildings. It was worth the prospect of an official telling-off, and an angry phone call to his parents; worth it to be back in the safe world where things would be in proportion once more, where someone else would know best what he should do.

The guard must have pressed a button or pulled a lever, for the gate opened. As the car slid slowly past him, David saw, briefly, a cheerful moon of a face beaming in at them. The car rolled on by. A door in the building directly ahead of them was already swinging upwards, but then, as the car slid into a slot of darkness, the door hesitated before swinging down again and closing tightly behind them. The car sighed, inching forward then coming at last to a standstill.

5

Immediately lights came on. They were in a square white box so neat and pure, it was hard to believe it was a mere garage. The sound of music came faintly from somewhere but, to David's great relief, there were no voices singing.

Then, as he stared around him, parallel black cracks appeared in the white wall directly in front of them and not one but two doors opened. The two black spaces in the white wall seemed to issue opposing orders. 'Go through me!' each door seemed to be commanding.

As Harley flung the driver's door wide, that music

came roaring in, twisting around them in ropes of sound.

'I'm not getting out,' said David.

Harley immediately shut himself in again, but he could not shut the music out. 'Oh, come on!' he begged. 'What are you scared of?'

'Electronic ghosts,' David muttered. 'What if the security system vaporizes us?'

'You said they do forestry research here,' said Harley uneasily. 'That's trees, right? They won't be worrying about tree security with us. What's the bet they'll just tell us off, and then drive us back onto the motorway and turn us loose?'

David was amazed at Harley's optimism.

'You're unreal,' he said wearily. 'I mean – think of this car. It's not just an average old taxi, is it? It's weird. The whole place is weird. Let's ... let's just ... just make some sort of a *plan*, and then maybe we can ... '

His voice trailed away and they both flopped back in their seats, studying those black doorways in front of them. As they stared blankly ahead, a figure appeared in the left-hand doorway.

One moment the doorway had been dark and empty. The next, someone was there, looking back at them. In spite of the shadows they could see her in totally unexpected detail: a girl older than they were – sixteen or seventeen, perhaps – a little hunched, hugging around her (as if her pockets were full of treasures) a disintegrating leather jacket that fell almost to her knees. Her hair, dyed bright red, was cropped close to her skull. Big, dark glasses with metal rims hid most of her face, but they could see three rings in her right ear and one in her left nostril. She was certainly not the kind of person you would expect to find in a forestry research establishment.

The boys stared at her, and she stared at them. Then she must have stepped back as quickly as she had stepped forward. Without giving any impression of moving, somehow she just wasn't there any more.

'Hey!' said Harley. 'Some chick!'

Obviously the sight of this girl had lifted his spirits a little, and he was trying to play it cool again.

'Okay,' said David, giving in. 'Let's face the music.'

'What music?' asked Harley. 'Mozart?'

'Oh, ha ha!' said David. 'There's bound to be some trouble, isn't there? I mean we did sort of *steal* this car.'

'It stole us!' Harley sounded almost pious. 'And, anyhow, anyone who leaves a car with the keys in it is *asking* to get it lifted.'

Harley's words bothered David. It was true. The car had almost been begging for theft and misuse.

And, as he thought this, someone tapped on the car window.

Harley let out a small, shrill, rodent cry. David didn't blame him for shrieking. He would have shrieked himself if his throat had not been paralysed by a new shock of terror. The sudden knock had sounded three inches from his ear. Turning, he looked into the beaming moon-face of the guard who had waved them through the gate. He must have come through some unseen door, and now he was peering in at them, still smiling.

Scrambling out of the car, David on one side, Harley on the other, they crouched slightly, ready for anything, even attack. The man, though, looked entirely friendly.

The air around them still rang with piped music, but it seemed quieter than it had been when Harley had first opened the car door. Half listening, David realized it was now classical music of some kind.

'Great run!' the man said, patting the car affectionately. 'Nice to meet you at last, though I feel I know you already. I've been monitoring your approach. My name's Finney – Winston Finney. Winnie Finney, they call me. So how did you enjoy your million-dollar ride?'

'Amazing,' said David. At least he tried to say it. He felt his lips moving but no sound struggled out from between them.

'Wicked!' croaked Harley, valiantly trying to be cool.

'I, personally, took it through its imprinting run,' said Winnie Finney fondly. He patted the car's battered flank again. 'And I tuned and set up the guiding beacons. Well, though we call them beacons, they're so small no one knows they're there. Not to mention the latest Japanese technology in the distance sensors, and in those bumpers. Touch-sensitive, even at speed. But I mustn't blind you with science. Let's concentrate on getting you two hooligans sorted out. This way!'

David and Harley grinned foolishly at each other as they followed him through the right-hand door. Their reception wasn't nearly as fierce as they had imagined it might be.

Just inside the door a huge figure stood, seemingly waiting to greet them. David's heart, already pounding, gave a sharp leap and he made what sounded like a cry of terror.

'It's only a statue,' said Harley, 'of someone about to bowl a ball.'

'Atlas with the world in his hand,' Winnie Finney told them, looking back over his shoulder. 'Come on! You can admire it later.'

He led them past the statue and, entering an elevator, he pressed a button. David craned to watch, determined to know which floor they were being taken to. But these buttons had no numbers, and it was impossible to tell how fast or how far they were going. All he could be sure of was that they were shooting down.

'Long way?' he asked.

'Oh, yes,' said Winnie Finney. 'There's much, much more to this place than meets the eye, you know.'

The lift stopped and the door slid sideways. White corridors curved away to either side of them.

'I'm afraid you won't be able to go home straight away,' Winnie Finney said. 'But never mind! I'll take you to a place where you can have a cup of coffee and put your feet up.'

'Will I be able to ring my mother?' asked David, remembering that she would be waiting up for him, drinking coffee and trying not to worry, yet growing unhappier with every moment.

Though Winnie Finney patted his shoulder and spoke in a comfortable voice, he did not actually answer David's question.

'Only the most important people ever get down to the level we're making for,' he said. 'You're being treated like celebrities.'

He pushed his hand into his pocket and pulled out something that looked to David like a gun. However, there was no report when Winnie Finney pressed the trigger, merely the sound of a lock unlocking itself. Yet another door swung open.

'Quickly!' Winnie Finney pushed Harley and David ahead of him, his long arms held out to either side in case either of them should decide to break away and run for it.

'Sorry to hurry you, but an alarm goes off if that particular door doesn't close within the minute,' Winnie Finney told them. 'Security!' he added as if that explained everything.

They passed along a narrow, bright passage and came out into a second corridor, painted in pale blue and curving rather more tightly than the one they had just left. Half a dozen people were moving rapidly towards them from the right, led by a man and a woman both wearing pale blue overalls and jackets. Behind this pair walked three elegantly dressed people, one of whom was propelling what seemed to be an electronic wheelchair flashing coloured lights at them, in which sat a bony old man wearing something like an oxygen mask. It was an unexpected sight, even in this place. Winnie Finney seemed surprised by it, too. He exclaimed to himself, then flung out one arm imperiously.

'Stand back! Let these people pass,' he said softly, but sharply.

'We'll make everything as comfortable for you as we possibly can, Mr Yee,' the woman in blue overalls was saying as they advanced. One of the three people answered in a language David did not understand. He seemed to be translating the woman's words aloud, perhaps to the man in the wheelchair. None of them glanced at Winnie Finney and the boys as they swept on by.

'We specialize,' said Winnie Finney, once the group had retreated around the curve of the corridor, 'in developing aids of various kinds for people who have suffered accidents – who can't get around as easily as you or I do. Now then! This way. You both look rather disreputable, but never mind. You'll have a chance to tidy yourselves before you meet Dr Fabrice.'

'Dr who?' asked Harley.

'Oh no! Not Dr Who,' said Winnie Finney beaming

as if Harley had made a good joke on purpose. 'Fabrice! A very talented man. Highly thought of in intellectual circles.'

'Really, we just want to go home,' said David as politely as he could. 'And I want to ring my mother.'

But Winnie Finney was pointing his opener at a door which obediently swung open. Skipping to one side, he gestured them in.

'If you just wait here,' he said, 'I'll have someone with you in two shakes of a lamb's tail. You'll probably have to take a few tests and fill out some forms. Security!'

'We aren't security risks,' said Harley quickly.

'Ah, but you aren't particularly reliable, are you?' said Winnie Finney. 'You can't be, or you wouldn't be here in the first place.'

'We're sorry,' said David. 'It was a big mistake. Can't we just ...'

'The difficulty about a place like this is that we have to be so very security conscious,' Winnie Finney interrupted him, still beaming. 'Dr Fabrice will be with you as soon as possible.'

The last thing David saw of him, before the door clicked shut, was a cheerfully winking eye. The music faded, but did not altogether disappear. It continued to sound like the voice of an alien insect caught in the mazes of his ear.

David and Harley were now in a pale blue room with tightly shut blue doors in three of its walls. Four chairs, upholstered in blue linen, were placed precisely around a low, glass table spread with magazines in various languages. In one corner of the room stood a television set which looked far too ponderous to show anything as light-hearted as soap operas or cartoons. In the opposite corner was a bench which supported a water dispenser with a plastic tap, and a coffee machine with paper cups beside it. David suddenly became aware of how thirsty he was. He went over to get himself a drink. Harley, though, leaped to test first one door, then another.

'None of them have got *handles*,' he said incredulously. 'We can't get out.'

'Did you think they'd let you wander around?' asked a voice – a girl's voice.

And there she was – the girl they'd seen in the garage doorway. It was hard to be sure of anything in a place like this, but David was sure she had not been in the room when they first came into it.

7

'How did you get in?' asked Harley.

'I've been waiting for you,' she answered. 'I knew they'd bring you here.'

'No, but how did you actually get in?' Harley persisted.

'Oh, I can come and go,' she answered carelessly.

She was still wearing her big, round, dark glasses, and still hugging the long black jacket around her, almost as if she were cold. This made David register how very warm it was down here. For all that, the girl seemed to be shivering. Her bare legs vanished into high, black, laced Doc Martens.

31

'Just tell us,' said Harley. 'How do we get out? I mean, supposing we have to.'

The girl smiled. She had very white teeth, pointed and foxy. 'How did you get in?' she asked, mimicking Harley, but not unkindly.

'We got into a car which – which wasn't ours,' Harley said.

'Oh, that car!' the girl replied, nodding and taking a packet of chewing gum from her coat pocket.

'We sort of borrowed it ... well, actually it borrowed us,' said David, watching her pop a piece of gum into her mouth. She wore black leather fingerless gloves, and she did not offer the packet of gum to either of them.

'Wow! Isn't technology wonderful,' she said. It wasn't a question.

'Is the door behind you unlocked?' asked Harley. 'Is that the way out?'

'In the end it is,' the girl said. She spoke in a careless voice, but there was something strange about her expression. Then she opened her mouth but, though she seemed to struggle to speak, no words came. 'I-I-I-I ...'

she stammered, then stopped. 'I don't seem to be able to tell you much,' she said at last, blinking rapidly and speaking easily once more. 'You'll have to guess.'

'Do you work here?' Harley asked, while David stared at her, puzzled at what someone so street punk could be doing in this high-tech place.

'I do, at present,' she said. 'I'll be moving on when I finish my assignment.'

'What is your assignment?' David asked, but Harley cut in over him.

'Why can't you tell us much? Is it top secret or something?'

'I just can't,' she said. 'There's some law against it. I have to fight laws all the time just to be here – laws of nature, that is.'

'Can you answer *any* questions?' David asked her.

'Yes, if you ask the right question, that is. Anyhow, you're halfway there, whether I answer it or not,' replied the girl.

'Do we just have to sit here and wait?' Harley said irritably.

'Are you bored?' she asked.

'No,' said Harley. 'But that's not the point.'

'Because if you are bored, you should find something to entertain yourselves with.' Her head turned a little so that her dark glasses appeared to focus on the television set in the corner. 'Why not watch a soapie?' Her voice was light, almost playful, as if she were giving riddling instructions. 'Better than nothing!'

David moved over to the set, then glanced back at her. She nodded once. Encouraged, he pressed the button that said Power. The screen sprang to life.

The image that formed was not in full colour, but neither was it in black-and-white. The shadows and darker details were various shades of blue.

What they saw was one of those empty, curving corridors, perhaps the very one along which they had walked only ten minutes earlier. They stared expectantly, but the corridor remained empty. No doors opened. Nothing happened.

'Bor-ing!' said the girl half-chanting. 'Change channels.'

'How?' David asked, but as he spoke he saw a remote control on top of the set, snatched it up, and clicked the single button.

Immediately the corridor faded, but other shapes came crowding through it as it disappeared. The new scene seemed familiar. Ten blue and white people were moving in a complicated reel through a room filled with equipment. And, there on the screen, David could make out whole ranks of similar screens, crossed and recrossed by blips, undulating lines and tight scribbles of light.

'That's like a – a hospital, isn't it?' Harley said. 'Some sort of an operating room.'

'It could be a tree hospital,' suggested the girl. 'What do you reckon?'

'Tell us, then, if you're so smart,' said Harley. He and David both looked from the girl to the screen, then back to the girl once more. She frowned and opened her mouth but for the second time she choked, and no words came.

'Find out for yourselves,' she said at last, stepping back with an indifferent shrug. 'It's your funeral. Just take it easy with the, with the – with the drinking.' Then she laughed as if she had made a joke.

David pressed the programme selector a third time. The image on the screen faded as another came through it, and to begin with he could not understand what he was seeing, though at the same time he felt he knew it well. Two figures were standing and staring at a screen. The backs were familiar, and surely the chairs – that table spread with magazines... David spun around to check the magazines on the table beside him. Harley yelped.

'It's you!' he cried. David looked quickly back at the screen, but, as he turned his head, the image on the screen turned too, so he did not – could not – meet his own eyes.

'It's us, isn't it?' Harley said, whispering now, and shivered.

David found he was shivering, as well. 'There must be a camera somewhere,' he said, staring up at the ceiling. 'Look!' He pointed up at a corner. 'That black thing like a round eye. They're spying on us.'

'They call it "monitoring",' said the girl. 'It sort of suggests they're taking care of you. And they will take care of you, too – if you're not more careful than they are, that is. Watch out for any – ' she seemed to struggle again, 'any – hospitality.'

The last word came out almost violently, as if the word she most needed had choked her and she had to say something else instead.

David pressed the button again.

This time they were looking into a large, tiled room lined along two walls with a continuous flow of stainless-steel sinks, and taps and steel refrigerators. Two steel tables stood in the centre of the room, but without the crowding of expensive equipment they had seen in the operating theatre. The third wall, only partly visible, seemed to be lined with steel drawers, all tightly closed. In one corner, David got the impression of an area screened with plastic screens, like something he had seen before. However, before he could organize his memory, the screen went blank, then filled with flickering snow.

'Hang on!' said Harley. 'Let me see that room again?'

'It's switched itself off,' said David, pressing the button over and over.

'Override command,' said the girl. 'Old Doctor Fabricate's trying to come through.' And she chuckled a strange, dark chuckle.

A very different sort of picture began forming on the screen. They were now seeing, in full television colour, an office with a big, well-ordered desk and a well-ordered man sitting behind it.

'Good evening,' said the man. He spoke with an accent, but David could not guess what country it suggested. 'I am Doctor Fabrice. I think you were told to expect me. Now, listen carefully, because I am going to tell you what to do next.'

8

Dr Fabrice was looking at them with severe scientific attention.

'I know you must be alarmed by your situation, but you have no cause to worry. In two minutes the door to the left of this screen will slide open. Go into the room beyond. You will find clean clothes adjacent to the shower. You will then move into the antiseptic environment we need to maintain, so after you have showered, please put on the uniforms provided.'

'I'm not dressing in any uniform,' Harley muttered.

'Failure to comply with this ruling will result in

coercion,' Dr Fabrice went on, in a voice without emotion. 'After you have gone through the process of disinfection, you will be interviewed and appropriately classified. Do remember that you are here entirely by your own choice, and be cooperative. Cooperation will be to your advantage.'

The screen went blank once more, and one of the doors opened invitingly.

'I suppose we'd better go,' David said. He turned to look at the girl and was filled, once more, with the peculiar feeling of having missed out on something – something important.

'When we saw ourselves on that screen ...' He hesitated, and she raised her eyebrows at him. 'Where were you?' he asked her. 'You were right beside us, but the camera didn't pick you up.'

'Oh well, maybe I know enough about this place to keep out of the reach of cameras,' she answered. 'There are spots in every room the cameras miss. Or maybe I have a secret skill, and just don't show.' And she laughed to herself.

'What's your name?' David asked, looking back over his shoulder even as he stepped through the door.

'Quinta!' she said. 'What's yours?'

The door slid shut before he could answer. There was no going back.

Quinta! thought David. *Where's Quinta?* That was the graffiti on the wall in Forbes Street.

'Harley ...' he began, and then fell silent.

They were confronted by a series of four shower alcoves which made David feel as if he were a sheep about to be dipped against his will. Anxious to seem mature and responsible and to impress any cameras that might be watching them, David and Harley both undressed, folding their clothes neatly, something that neither of them did at home. Naked, they moved into separate shower alcoves. But, as they entered, shower doors closed behind them, clicking and locking in what was now a familiar fashion. Warm water smelling of disinfectant shot down on them so briskly it was like being bombarded with pins. When the showers stopped, what had appeared to be the back wall slid aside. First Harley, then David, came out – dripping and trembling – into a tiny room, tiled in blue and white, and without a single window.

There came a hiss, as a warm, greenish spray fell from sprinklers in the ceiling above them. The room smelled of another kind of antiseptic.

'They're disinfecting us.' Harley was outraged. 'What's going on?'

'He told us we would be disinfected,' David replied. 'That Dr Fabrice, I mean.' His voice sounded calm, but his head was spinning with amazement. *Quinta*, he was thinking. *Quinta!* She had, apparently, disappeared from Forbes Street. Her name had been written up there. *Where's Quinta?* the graffiti had asked over and over again. Could she have taken that car just as they had? How long had she actually been here?

A door hummed open. Yet another pale blue room. David glanced at the corners of the ceiling. Yes! There was the round, black eye of a camera. Someone was watching – still watching; someone was monitoring them. Pale blue towels and clothes were laid out on a steel bench.

'Dresses!' Harley was outraged.

'Gowns!' said David. 'Hospital gowns. At least they're blue, not pink!'

'I'm not wearing a thing like that!' said Harley. 'It'll show my bum.'

'No, it won't. Well, not quite. And I want to get this over and done with,' David said wearily, though the short gown did make him feel silly and defenceless. The door at the end of the room opened on cue. They walked through and found themselves in the well-ordered office they had first seen on the television set.

The man behind the desk looked at them pleasantly enough.

'So,' he said mildly. 'You stole a car and here you are.'

'We weren't really stealing it,' mumbled Harley.

'Just borrowing it?' suggested Dr Fabrice. 'Well, it's all very regrettable, but nothing we can't fix. It will take time. After all, you've pushed your way into a private establishment.'

'I thought Willesden Forest was run by the government,' Harley protested.

'Private in the sense that we don't encourage anyone to come here except by invitation,' the doctor said. 'Work goes on here which must be protected. We do have competitors, you know.'

'May I ring my mother – just to let her know I'm safe?' asked David.

'Certainly not,' Dr Fabrice replied calmly.

'She'll be off her head by now,' David cried.

'You should have thought of her before you got into that car.' Dr Fabrice sounded bored. 'However, you're lucky in one way. We don't want to prosecute, but we *will* need to monitor you for a short term. Goodness knows what problems you have brought in with you, and you may even have suffered some contamination, though we are as scrupulously careful as possible. So we must check you out – not that we actually want the extra work.'

'Contamination? You mean *viruses* might have got into us?' Harley was dismayed. 'Dangerous ones?'

'Let's hope not,' Dr Fabrice said. 'It is just possible, however. I'll give you the appropriate shots in a moment. In the meantime there are a few questions I'd like you to answer. Let's begin with your names and your dates of birth.'

Harley and David answered question after question. What illnesses had they had? Did they have any allergies? Were either of them taking any medications? Did either or both of them take drugs? Were either of them on insulin? Or steroids of any kind? Did they drink? Had either of them ever had any heart disease? Had either of them ever had any injections into the heart? Were there any illnesses in their families – illnesses they might have inherited? Nothing neurological? No kidney or liver malfunction?

The questions went on and on. David and Harley answered and answered until the room faded around them and they wilted in their chairs.

Finally Dr Fabrice rang a bell. A dark, young woman in a nurse's uniform came in pushing a small trolley. She did not so much as glance at the boys. It was as if they did not exist.

'We need a blood sample from each of you,' said Dr Fabrice. 'It won't hurt.'

'What's all this in aid of?' Harley demanded yet again.

'It's for your own good,' Dr Fabrice repeated. 'It's not worth explaining. You wouldn't understand why.' His voice was soft and calm, but there was something unpleasant – even insulting – about it, too.

'We're not stupid,' David said, watching his blood climb out of the needle and into the tube the nurse was holding.

Dr Fabrice glanced at him.

'Are you not?' he asked. 'Then why are you here? You were not invited.'

'Okay, so it was a dumb thing to do,' David said. 'But everyone does something stupid sooner or later.'

'A charming theory.' Dr Fabrice smiled coldly.

'Hang on a bit,' David began, suddenly wanting to argue.

But Harley began jiggling nervously beside him, muttering, 'Shut up! Shut up!' under his breath. Then he said aloud, 'We're sorry. Okay? We'll go away and never bother you again – never say another word. Promise!'

'Of course, I do believe you,' said Dr Fabrice in his wintery voice. 'Of course, I entirely believe you'll walk away and never so much as *whisper* about anything you may have seen here. Two boys as honest as you would stick to your promises, I am sure. All the same, the foolish rules insist that you sign these forms – legal agreements to remain silent about your little misadventure. This is a research facility, you know. And these are the days of international industrial espionage. So … sign these forms, and then we can hold you legally responsible for any rumours in the world out there.'

'Do you think we're spies?' asked Harley incredulously. 'But we're … we're just … just kids.'

'But many people of your age are well able to communicate – to manipulate computers, for example,' said Dr Fabrice. 'Sign those forms now and, later, after we have checked with our lawyer, you will probably be sent home.'

'Probably!' exclaimed Harley.

'How much later?' asked David. 'I mean, my mother – please let me ring her.'

'I'm afraid not,' said Dr Fabrice, watching as Harley signed the pink form without bothering to read it.

Then it was David's turn. As he scribbled his signature he heard Harley yawning behind him, and knew exactly how he felt. It seemed as if they were signing off after a long and dangerous job, free, at last, to feel properly tired, even sleepy.

Dr Fabrice took the forms and put them in a basket on one side of his desk.

'I can offer you a bed until ... oh, until the morning shift comes on,' he said. 'I suggest you sleep. Our night staff will wash and clean your clothes for you.'

Dr Fabrice sounded so sure of what must be done.

The worst was over. Sleep would somehow make the next few hours come and go in less than a second.

David and Harley looked at each other, half-nodding, half-shrugging.

Sitting beside his desk, Dr Fabrice had seemed imposing; on his feet he was revealed as short and squat. The boys followed him out into the corridor, and once again music came to meet them. More than meet – it assailed them. To David it sounded like the music that had been playing when they first stepped out of the elevator into this pale blue curve. For some reason it made him think, as it had then, of horror films – of mad, hooded figures sitting in front of double keyboards, with stops and pipes sprouting like alien fungi from solid rock.

Dr Fabrice opened a door. They were looking into yet another room, but this time David saw whiteness: two white beds, so soft and pure that an involuntary sigh of pleasure escaped him at the sight. After the shower, the disinfecting, then the question-and-answer session, he felt soft and pure himself, all natural dirt washed away from his skin and out of his head, and all responsibility passed on. He and Harley let Dr Fabrice herd them into the room, and David, glancing upwards, checked for any lensed eye that might be scanning the room. Yes! There it was, still watching him. But so what? All it would see, over the next few hours, would be two boys sleeping, free of care.

And then Harley cried out in terror.

David's gaze skidded across Harley's gaping face to the bed on the left-hand side of the narrow room. It had been empty. It *had*! Yet now there was someone in it.

A young man lay on his back under the crisp white cover, apparently asleep. David thought, in that first dizzy second, that he was wearing long, fingerless, blue lace gloves, then understood that the hands (folded left over right) were covered in intricate tattoos. His forearms writhed with flowers, naked girls half covered in their own flowing hair, and spiralling serpents. The skin showing between the lines looked yellowish and translucent, the flesh like rapidly clearing water. *If I keep looking*, David thought in terror, *I'll be able to see right through him to the sheet beneath.* The room seemed to fall away, and for a moment he believed, with woolly astonishment, that he was about to faint. *I can't! I mustn't*, he thought, twisting around to stare at Dr Fabrice, standing behind him. For a moment Dr Fabrice appeared to have a ghastly owl perched on his shoulder. Familiar dark glasses were staring at David from just behind the doctor, who seemed entirely unaware of either the young man in the bed, or Quinta, his close shadow.

Harley screamed again. A horrid scarlet had begun pumping up between the man's fingers, spreading over the thin, blue border of the white sheet.

'Blood!' Harley shouted.

'Now, then,' Dr Fabrice said, staring at them in irritation. 'Don't make a stupid fuss. Sleep – just sleep – and we'll wake you for breakfast.'

Behind him, Quinta straightened as if she were a puppet jerked upwards by unseen strings. Tilting back her head, she howled: 'Run! Run now! There's no waking up! No breakfast! Hide! Hi–ide! Run and hide!'

Dr Fabrice may not have been able to see the young man and the flow of blood, but he heard Quinta – that owl looking over his shoulder. Suddenly he knew she was there. His jaw dropped, he turned; Quinta actually smiled at him as if they were old friends. His eyes were only inches away from her glasses. As David and Harley, acting together, pushed past him, a dreadful sound forced its way out of Dr Fabrice: not just a groan of fear, but the agony of a man feeling his brain invisibly twisting inside his head. First Harley, then David, scrambled past him and out of the room, pelting as fast as they could along the pale blue, curving corridor, even though they knew of no safe place to run to. It was as if they had been practising that fast take-off for a long time, and must make use of it, come what may.

Behind the perpetual music something began screaming. *Someone's torturing a cat*, thought David in horror, but the sound rose and fell too evenly for true pain, always incoherent. He realized he was hearing a siren – an alarm call. Glancing back over his shoulder, he saw Dr Fabrice crawling on the floor of the blue corridor with his head hanging almost to the floor, as a mechanical toy with a broken neck might crawl. Then he collapsed and lay still. David felt certain that, though Dr Fabrice might get up again, he would never be the same man he had been.

And now David also felt the vibration of pursuit. Feet were running from somewhere, pounding towards them. Grabbing a handle on the nearest door, he twisted it madly. Miraculously, the door opened, and he and Harley leaped sideways into darkness, pulling the door shut behind them. It clicked in such a conclusive way that David immediately knew they were locked in again, and the thought of being locked in this unknown, black room made him giddy with fear. Who knew what was in such a room, sharing the darkness with them? As he sank down on his trembling haunches, burying his face in his hands, he was aware of Harley collapsing beside him.

'He was dead. That man in the bed was dead,' Harley mumbled. David suspected he might be weeping in the dark.

'Shhh!' he whispered. Feet thumped rapidly past the door. David put out his hand and touched Harley's arm.

'He can't have been dead.' He wanted to be sensible and comforting at the same time. 'Dead men don't bleed like that. I mean, if he was dead his heart would have stopped beating and ... '

'He was dead,' repeated Harley. 'And not only that ...'

He fell silent. David did not want to think about what Harley had started to say. Before entering the previous room, they had looked in at the beds, and those beds had certainly been empty.

As if it were feeding on David's fear, the music grew louder and louder. The darkness rang with it, and David felt that he was ringing with it, too.

10

Then it faded again.

'I hate that music,' panted David.

'Bach!' whispered Harley.

'Bark?' David turned his head towards Harley, but could see only blackness. 'Woof woof?'

'Bach! You know. Bach, the composer. They've been playing that ever since we came in here. And Mozart, I think. Nothing but organ music anyway.'

It vaguely surprised David that Harley knew about composers and organ music. But he had probably heard a lot of music from his mother.

'What *happened*?' Harley sounded stern, like someone struggling out of a nightmare, desperate to take control of life once more.

'Quinta yelled "Run!" and we ran,' David said. He took a deep breath. 'Harley … you know that street where we found the car? Forbes Street?'

Harley nodded.

'Quinta's name was sprayed on the wall there. "Where's Quinta?" it said. Well, Quinta's *here*. But what's she doing here?'

He felt Harley shrug in the darkness. 'What are *we* doing here?' he replied.

'It's not the same,' said David. 'Not yet, anyway,' he added, shuddering as he spoke. 'We've just arrived, and she must have been here for a long time. She knows her way around.'

'She knew about the car too,' Harley agreed.

'We were tricked here. That car was a trap,' said David. 'I think it's sent out into Forbes Street to catch people. When people see it with the keys in it, they're tempted. Maybe that's why Forbes Street has such a bad name.

But why? I mean, who'd spend a million dollars on a car with a brain of its own, just to catch kids like us? It's like a dream: some moments I feel like I almost know what's going on, but then it fades before I can grab hold of it.'

He waved his hand in the dark. 'I mean, when you mentioned organ music a minute ago it seemed like you'd said something really important – but I don't know why. Ghostly!'

'Sshh! Don't talk about ghosts in here,' said Harley. His voice was still trembling, but he was beginning to sound more like his usual sharp self.

'I don't believe in ghosts,' David retorted. 'I never have! All the same…' he began, and stopped. It was mad, but he had to say it. 'Talking about ghosts…'

'Yeah, yeah!' Harley interrupted him, leaping to his feet and kicking something that rang like a tin bell. 'Where are the lights?'

David heard him scrabbling around the wall beside the door.

'There must be lights somewhere. Ah! Here we are…'

The burst of powerful white light made David feel he had been struck in the face.

They were in a large, bright room, hemmed around by stainless steel benches, sinks and steel-doored refrigerators. The floor and even the walls were covered with white tiles, though one wall was patched with big gleaming drawers. In the centre of the room stood two spotless steel tables with channels in them, and beyond these was an alcove largely closed off by pleated plastic screens. David had never been in this room before. All the same, he recognized it. It had appeared on the waiting-room television set. He looked up at the ceiling and, sure enough, there was the camera's familiar black eye staring down at them. David remembered that the plastic screens had been on the edge of the eye's field of sight, and Quinta had said that there were some spots in every room which the camera could not see.

'Let's hide behind those screens,' he said. 'Come on.'

'Why would anyone come all the way out here for an operation?' Harley asked. 'I mean – why would they?'

59

'I don't know,' said David, as they edged uneasily towards the screens. 'Maybe because they don't want to go on long waiting lists at ordinary hospitals. But hang on, this isn't an operating theatre.'

'It must be. Those tables …'

'It's more of a … a mortuary,' said David. 'I've seen them on TV.' He grimaced as he glanced around, then lowered his voice in case he disturbed some intangible presence. 'They pull out one of those drawers and there's your wife or someone they've dredged up out of the river,' he whispered.

'A mortuary?' Harley muttered back, his voice alive with new alarm. 'Why would they want one out here?'

David edged behind the screens, listening to the music.

'Organ music.' His teeth which had been clenched until now began to chatter. 'Organ music,' he repeated. 'And something being done secretly. There's something creepy going on …'

They turned and found themselves facing an arched doorway and a little room with narrow beds where two people lay – alone, but not unattended. Each bed was so surrounded by machines and screens that the room was like the setting for a science-fiction game. The occupants lay like dead people, but the looping lines on the screens beside the beds seemed to indicate that some sort of monitored life was being lived by the people stretched out there.

'Think about it,' he said slowly, staring at the screens. 'What if Dr Fabrice does secret medical deals for rich people – swapping organs or whatever. Some people have to wait a long time for a new heart.' Then his mind made another jump. 'And what if ...'

'Shut up!' Harley snapped. 'Let's just get out of here.'

The patient in the nearest bed was the young man they had already seen in the bed further down the hall. There was no doubt about it. Though he now had a mask on, with various tubes and wires plastered into his neck and arms, the blue tattoos on his hands and forearms were unmistakable. His skin was pale but lacked the horrid transparency it had before. David felt suddenly sure that he had materialized in front of them to give them some

sort of warning. And in the next bed … the next bed …
He must see who was under that sheet, wired into the
machines. He felt sure it was Quinta.

'Don't look!' Harley guessed what David was about
to do.

And then they heard a quiet sound. Beyond the
screens the door had opened.

'Are you there?' someone asked in a loud whisper.
'You can come out now.'

Harley put a finger to his lips. But feet were crossing
the tiled floor. 'Don't be worried,' said the voice. 'I'm on
your side.'

Someone peered around the screens, and beamed at
them. 'Oh, there you are!'

It was the gatekeeper, Winnie Finney.

11

'A lot of people are looking for you two,' he remarked. 'I thought I'd join in the hunt. You seem to be causing a bit of trouble, and I have a soft spot for trouble-makers. I was a bit of a tearaway myself, way back when.'

'Something's going on,' said David. 'Something really freaky.'

Winnie Finney looked around the room, rather as if he too found it unpleasant.

'After all, it *is* a research establishment,' he said, half to himself. 'No wonder people like you and me find it all a bit strange ... a little bit bothering, I mean to say.

And I can't believe you kids mean any harm. So if we get to my room you can hide out there, until the daytime staff come on duty. You'll have more chance of getting away when there are a lot of people around. They won't pick you out in the same way.'

David could have kissed him. He sounded so ordinary and easy going … so *reliable*.

'I'll check the corridor,' said Winnie Finney. 'The elevator's almost directly opposite.'

The boys watched as he opened the door, peered right, peered left, and then beckoned them forward.

'Are you ready? Then follow me. Now!'

Sliding furtively after him, a little way along the blue corridor, they stopped beside a dark blue grill. Winnie Finney pressed a button. First the grill, and then the door behind it, hissed open. The three of them piled through, Winnie Finney pressing buttons. The elevator shot down (though how far down David could not tell), then came to a stop. The door slid open once more, and they stepped out on to a deep red carpet. The warm colour was a relief after all that chilly blue.

'My office is along here,' said Winnie Finney. 'And no one bothers to bother me. I'm the mechanic – the odd-jobs man. So come and sit down and have something to eat. Then you can tell me what's going on.'

'I'm starving,' said Harley, which amazed David, for he couldn't imagine ever wanting to eat anything ever again. The mere thought of meat made his stomach heave painfully. He was thirsty, but all he wanted to drink was water. More than anything else, he wanted things to be simple and ordinary once more.

Winnie Finney led the way along the red carpet to a polished door which opened into a book-lined room, worn and homely. He had an untidy desk, an overflowing wastepaper basket, and an old-fashioned bar heater. There was a table in one corner of the room, on which sat an old electric jug. Shelves rose behind it with cups and saucers and a tin that looked as if it might hold biscuits.

'Sit!' said Winnie Finney, as if they were dogs. 'Just for a moment. Are you cold?' He leaned behind his desk to turn on the heater. 'We'll be warm as toast in a minute.'

David slumped gratefully into a cane chair filled with soft, floppy cushions.

'I'll lock the door,' said Winnie Finney. 'Then no one will be able to burst in on us.' And he did.

'Now tell me everything,' he said to David, 'while I make coffee.'

'Well,' David began, 'we were walking home ... hours ago, it was –'

'Last night,' Harley put in. 'Or maybe it was tonight. Weird. Time seems to have stretched out or collapsed or something.'

'Whichever it was,' said David, looking at the windows. Between a slit in the drawn curtains he saw what looked like a genuine night-time darkness, and, slightly darker and thicker than that darkness, branching fingers ... part of a tree. They must be close to ground level once more.

Between them they told Winnie Finney about finding the car with the winking, seductive key, and the way they had been carried along the motorway and over the hill. As they talked, Winnie Finney made the coffee, and set the low table with biscuits and three wide, flowery cups. He poured coffee into the cups, then, with a roguish look, took a silver hip flask from his pocket and added a slug of ginger-coloured liquid to each.

'We're all men of the world,' he said. 'We need something for shock. Help yourselves to milk and sugar.'

He sat back in what was obviously his special chair. It had lions' heads on the arms, and he hung his hands across them so that the lions seemed to be snarling out from between his wide fingers.

By now Harley and David were talking about Quinta, the ghost in dark glasses, interrupting one another as they talked, filled with the relief of passing on their fears, and the pleasure of being in an ordinary room filled with ordinary things. In between talking, Harley took his first sips of coffee quite greedily, evidently enjoying it, relaxing with feeling of grown-up, manly fellowship. David, too, took a sip of the coffee, but thought it tasted unpleasant.

Too strong, he thought. *Too much of something*. He stood, wriggling his shoulders, and began moving restlessly around the room. Winnie Finney watched him curiously.

'I feel a bit too screwed-up about things,' David said. 'I can't just sit there! But can you tell me … this isn't just a forestry place, is it? I mean it might be, but there's something else going on here.' He held his coffee cup in both hands, as if he were enjoying its warmth and comfort.

'Transplants!' announced Harley, as proudly as if he had worked it out for himself. David looked over at him in surprise, for he didn't think Harley had even listened to his theory. 'They pick up people on the streets, and David thinks they use them for spare parts. I mean, sometimes people just vanish, don't they? And no one's going to report that car missing. In a way, it doesn't exist. In an official way that is. It won't be registered. It's an invention, that car. You get into it and you disappear.'

Winnie Finney looked at Harley, his smile vanishing.

'It is possible,' he said. 'I designed that car, you know.

My main work is unmanned machines – machines that are used in hard-access forestry areas. The car was just a hobby, a treat. And once I'd solved the problems, set it up with a homing device and so on, I rather lost interest. And it's true that some of the people I see around here from time to time don't look like your average tree lovers.'

Finding himself unobserved, David tipped his coffee into a pot plant.

'What do tree lovers look like?' Harley asked with a faint grin, his first for quite a while. He sounded relaxed, even sleepy. At the same time, the coffee cup fell from his fingers, spreading what was left of the coffee across the floor. Alarmed, David took a step forward trying to check on Harley whose small movements seemed to have become enormously slow and ponderous. Winnie Finney nodded at Harley, and then swung sideways in his chair to look at David. Instinctively, David half-closed his eyes, and moved back towards his chair, pretending to stumble a little, while Winnie Finney beamed at him across his own untouched cup of coffee. This man, who had seemed so friendly, so much on their side, had offered them drugged coffee. David forced a thick, wordless sound between his lips.

'Ah, I see you've caught on,' said Winnie Finney, leaning forward and peering intently at David, rather as if his face was the page in a book and he was reading it. 'You *know*, don't you?' His mouth stretched into an even wider smile.

Harley was looking slowly from one to the other of them.

'What's ... wrong?' he asked, and his voice sounded even slower and more smudgy.

David did not reply. Inside his head he felt sharp and in charge, but he must hide it. Best if Winnie Finney thought he was dealing with two drugged and dim-witted young men. He collapsed back into his chair.

Winnie Finney rose briskly and stood over them.

'There are so many worthless people around,' he said, suddenly transformed: still beaming, but no longer kindly. 'Yet these worthless ones – these trashy people – have perfectly good organs: lungs, hearts, livers … while there are worthwhile citizens, people who have lived good, productive lives, or lovely youngsters with a world of promise ahead of them, who, simply through some silly accident of fate, find their bodies breaking down. Properly functioning organs should not be wasted on scum who are going to vandalize themselves with drink and drugs.'

He wandered across his little office, studied a barometer on the wall and tapped it delicately. Then he turned back to the boys.

'The two young men in the room off the morgue are what we call "brain-dead",' he said. 'They would certainly die if we disconnected them from the life-support systems you saw, but we are keeping them alive – technically alive. We need them fresh, you see. They don't deserve to live. They didn't respect themselves so why should someone like me bother to respect them?'

Winnie Finney laughed. 'But so many organs can have a useful life, once they are taken from the parent body. A heart should be transposed within six to eight hours. A lung may last for twelve hours. Of course there are parts of the body that can be preserved. Freshly frozen skin can last for over three years. So can bone marrow. Heart valves last for five years and so does the cartilage of the knee. We'll use those young men with far more respect and dignity than they would have used themselves, even though comparatively little of them will be usable. Their corneas (from their eyes, you know), their lungs, perhaps ... Some sections of skin. Now *you* – provided you don't have leukaemia, AIDS risk factors, or anything of that kind – you are treasure troves. At your age you're not likely to have fluid in the lungs, or pancreatic malfunction.'

He frowned at them, looking a little troubled.

'You see, once you're here there's no going back,' he said with irritation. 'There can't be. Why on earth were you stupid enough to get into the car? It was a dishonest thing to do, and you both know it. What were you doing in Forbes Street, of all disgusting places?'

David did not answer. He felt sure that, if he did, Winnie Finney would realize he was much sharper than he was pretending to be. But there was some truth in what Winnie Finney was saying. He and Harley had deliberately climbed into a car that was not theirs. They had driven away in it: a dishonest thing to do. They didn't deserve whatever was about to happen to them, and yet in the beginning it had been their fault. *Never again!* He found himself thinking. *If we get out of this … well, never again.*

'I was a Forbes Street kid,' said a voice – Quinta's. Yet she was not in the room. Her voice was in David's head. 'I had my tattoos done in Forbes Street. I had my ears pierced there. I was trash – or that's what he would have called me. But I was tough trash. Too tough for him! He hasn't been able to see me off. I'm still hanging round, waiting for my chance.'

Winnie Finney seemed quite unaware that Quinta was speaking. He was still talking about organs: 'There are better people than you who can use your corneas, your livers and tendons. You'll both have profoundly fulfilled lives. And, after all, it is immortality of a kind.'

He picked up his phone.

'Call me! Go on, call me!' said Quinta's voice. 'Make him see me!'

David could not speak, but he shouted with a soundless voice he discovered within himself.

'Quinta! *Quinta!*'

'I have with me the two specimens we mislaid,' Winnie Finney was saying into the phone. 'They're in good condition except for a sleeping drug that will work its way through their systems quite harmlessly. But we've been a little complacent, haven't we? A little careless?' His words were mild but his voice was somehow menacing. He was being nasty to someone. 'We must be careful,' he said.

David made himself shudder. He probably overdid it, trembling furiously, but Winnie Finney did not seem suspicious. And he did not seem to notice that behind him the air was swirling and thickening.

Quinta was forming herself out of nothing.

Of course! David thought. *She really is a ghost. She isn't chained to any life-support system.* All the same, he definitely did not believe in ghosts. He had never believed in them, even when he was a little boy.

'Stop thinking me out of existence,' Quinta's voice said. 'Think at him! *At* him! *At* him! They can't monitor thoughts. They can't transplant ideas. Tell him *he's* the blemished one! Sullied! Disfigured! Load me with words. I'll use them like bullets! I can! You can! You *must*.'

Having that voice in his head was like looking into a dreadful mirror and seeing a monster smiling back at him. At the same time he felt a sense of power stir in him, and that power was his. Quinta's presence had set something free. He could use words, not just for fun but as if they were weapons. He tried desperately to think of fierce words he could invent.

'Cantankerous! Cantakofulum! *Furioso*!' he cried, firing the words off violently, and sensing that Quinta would snatch them out of the air, give them mysterious force, and shoot them at Winnie Finney – who abruptly stopped his conversation and looked at him with annoyance.

'Shut up!' said Winnie Finney. 'I'm on the phone.'

'Snarlarium! Fang-Fang!' yelled David, inventing desperately. Bullets! Yes! He was certainly firing those words out into the room and once he had turned them loose, Quinta had the power – a sort of ghost power – to use them as actual weapons. He certainly wouldn't have been able to invent words, let alone fire them, if he had drunk that drugged coffee. He glanced at the pot plant and saw that the poor thing had collapsed and tumbled out of its pot. Meanwhile Harley was struggling to stay awake. But then Harley met his eyes and made a clumsy gesture. Clumsy or not he was trying to point to the door. Within himself, David heard music – the same music that had haunted the corridor outside.

'Fire the words!' Quinta ordered him. 'Send them through me. I'll give them dominance – I'll give them substance. I'm nothing but a dream now … a sort of dream … but I'm a dream set free, and free dreams have power.'

'Yes! Yes! Call a team together!' Winnie Finney was saying, but he was starting to stammer a little. 'Call a … call … call … ' Then he stiffened, dropped the phone, and swung around to stare at David.

David immediately began trying to remember all the fierce words he knew. 'Avenge! Avengalatum!' he shouted – remembering, then inventing.

Winnie Finney took a step towards him.

'Avengalatum!' hissed Quinta, an echo that only David could hear, and the word flew from her like a bullet from a gun.

Winnie Finney stopped and stood staring at David, swaying as if he had been struck. Behind him, Harley seemed to revive a little, sitting up in his chair, then standing unsteadily.

'Devastation! Bashaboutabit!' screamed David, and felt Quinta seize his words and fire them at Winnie Finney, whose knees began to tremble. The words were knocking him about. Harley looked just as unsteady on his feet, but David could tell at once that Harley had a plan. He must keep Winnie Finney from turning around.

'What are you trying to say?' Winnie Finney demanded. 'Speak clearly!'

'I am a master of words,' David was thinking fast. 'Destructosaurus!' He began to chant:

> *Destructosaurus!*
>
> *Ichthyosaurus*
>
> *Tyrannosaurus* Rex!

Harley was almost at the door, staggering but silent.

'Oh no!' Winnie Finney said softly, staring from side to side as if voices came from all directions.

Harley! thought David. Harley, even drugged and stumbling, was joining in the crazy chant, and the ghostly Quinta was using it to absorb all Winnie Finney's attention. Perhaps there were other voices, too, that David couldn't hear, though the room seemed to ring with echoes. People might have died in this room, but now David's words were bringing some part of them to life again, and those voices from the past were growing powerful.

Behind Winnie Finney, Harley struggled to turn the key in the lock.

'Dastardly! Diabolical!' cried David. 'Snarlopendous! Gnashgnash! Gnashgnash!' He hissed these words ferociously, and Quinta seemed to spin, arms wide, gathering the words and gaining strength from them. Winnie Finney threw up one arm as if defending himself from a blow.

Then two things happened: Harley pushed the door wide, stumbling then falling through it, and Winnie Finney's face grew pale, the colour of uncooked pastry.

'You!' he shouted. 'You're dead. Don't you look at me like that! My little girl was worth a hundred of you. You know very well that since she died, I've *helped* humanity – those that deserved it. I've only used villains and useless wretches of the world. Humanity's garbage!'

Quinta was looking at him fixedly. David could only see the red stubble on the back of her head – a skull sprinkled with cayenne pepper.

'You're being paid though, aren't you?' she said to Winnie Finney. 'You don't give our parts away. You've made a fortune.' She tilted her glasses so that she and Winnie Finney stood, apparently, eye to eye.

Winnie Finney screamed like a tormented man.

Fool! Stupid fool! thought David. *Go on! Set us free!* 'Fall down!' he shouted aloud. 'Roll over!' Winnie Finney dropped obediently to his knees.

'Come on!' Harley was scrambling unsteadily onto his hands and knees. He called in a strange, thick voice, 'Now!'

David leaped between Quinta and Winnie Finney toward the door.

'Funny, though! I can see right through you!' Quinta was saying, laughing a little as she spoke. 'These boys here – I'm using their energy, their *force*, their *words* as weapons. I'm working through them.'

Winnie Finney screamed again.

David paused in the open doorway. He couldn't help it. He had to know what would happen next.

'Come *on!*' yelled Harley, already trying to turn the door handle.

As David watched, a slow, dark slug undulated over the curve of Quinta's cheek. As if she were about to speak to him, she turned her head slowly towards him. Light struck the slug, showing it a rich, thick red colour.

With her dark glasses still tilted up on her forehead, she looked directly at him.

Quinta had no eyes. They had been cut out of her head. Below those two ragged caves her smile was horrifying.

'Rubbish off the street!' screamed Winnie Finney, rolling on the floor at her feet. He had wriggled back against his desk. 'I gave your eyes to someone who uses them properly – a wonderful artist.'

Quinta laughed. 'I don't hold it against you,' she said. 'How can I? After all, you have my heart. Frozen!' She let the top of her coat fall open. Her bare chest was revealed, like some sort of winter seed pod, cracked open and empty. 'My heart and more besides.' She wrenched the coat wide. The whole body it had concealed seemed to split open, tumbling tubes and pieces that nobody could use – that nobody had wanted – on to the floor between them.

Winnie Finney writhed and struggled, collapsing still further, as if air were escaping from him.

'Oh, what a piece of work is man,' said Quinta. 'Woman, too!'

'Come on!' yelled Harley from the doorway.

Winnie Finney began gasping as if he would never get air into his lungs again. His heels beat up and down on the floor, kicking over his rubbish basket. Crumpled paper spilled out as if it were anxious to be free. His hands slapped the polished boards in desperation. His gasping gave way to a kind of wet, dirty gurgling. At last he lay still.

Quinta carelessly patted her dark glasses back into place. Smoke was rising behind her. David thought it was part of her ghostliness – a special effect with dry ice, perhaps.

'He could have done with a better heart himself, couldn't he?' she remarked. 'I don't suppose I *was* much, back when I was alive, and probably the people who wound up with my eyes, my liver, my kidneys – all my bits – made better use of them than I would have. But I reckon you ought to offer your own eyes before you start volunteering other people's, don't you? I was determined to get him. But until you two walked in and I found someone who could believe in ghosts, nothing worked.

I really pulled myself together when you two came along. And Scag, that guy with the tats, Fabrice and Finney did the same thing to him that they did to me – turned him into a desirable product hooked up to machinery so they could use pieces of him when they needed to. But they're both dead themselves now. And now I'm off. I don't know what comes next, and I don't care. Whatever it is, it'll be a good change.'

As David stared, Quinta grew transparent. She became nothing but patches of colour in the air. Her dark glasses, hiding the empty eye sockets, hung on for a little, staring out at the world. Then she vanished.

'Come *on*!' yelled Harley again. His voice was thick and strange. 'I'm going to go to sleep if I don't move. Come now!'

Suddenly David realized that papers on the floor were blazing. Winnie Finney had kicked the contents of the rubbish basket into his heater. The basket itself was on fire, and the desk was starting to burn. The room began to fill with smoke, along with a nasty smell of melting plastic. David coughed and spluttered as he turned and ran, smoke following. Behind him the flames leapt higher.

We'll never get out, thought David, but suddenly, like blessings from above, overhead sprinklers came on. David toppled himself forward, falling beside Harley. Smoke was curled after him.

'This way,' mumbled Harley. 'Ground floor.' But he just stood there, doing nothing.

'Don't go to sleep!' yelled David, getting back onto his feet and shaking him. 'Not now! You can't! You didn't drink all that coffee. You spilled a lot of it.'

Smoke shifted in the air around them. It almost seemed as if Winnie Finney's ghost was moving in the air around them, anxious to escape. Then David, peering past Harley, made out a shape blurred with darkness, just ahead of them.

'There's someone waiting there,' he coughed. 'Someone huge!' David's heart seemed to stop beating for a moment, but then he remembered. 'It's that statue!' he cried. 'The door must be somewhere over there.'

And it was. Moments later they were out of the great

white spaceship-building, standing on a street. People were running towards them.

'Where can we hide?' hissed Harley, but these people were not interested in them. It was the smoke billowing through overhead windows, the flicker of flames inside the building that had caught their attention. One man saw them, slowed down and stopped.

'What's going on? What have you done?' he asked.

'We haven't done anything,' said David, and for that moment, at least, it seemed quite true. An enormous relief was taking hold of him. It began in the pit of his stomach and moved up through him as if coals inside him were giving out black smoke like the smoke billowing through the second floor windows. Harley fell on his knees and then lay on the ground, and David, feeling the outside world blur and close in on him, tumbled down beside him. Somewhere out in the distance a robot wolf began howling – and then another one. Fire engines must be on the way.

12

'Dr Finney – that man Winnie Finney – wasn't a medical doctor,' said David's mother, perching on the side of his bed. 'He was some sort of engineer specializing in very sophisticated automated machines for use in forestry operations. Unfortunately, something terrible happened to him. He was a widower with one child – a daughter whom he adored – and this poor girl had a faulty heart. She was on a waiting list for a transplant operation, but while she was waiting she died, and apparently her death pushed Dr Finney over the edge, as they say.'

'Anyhow,' said David's father, 'when that overseas conglomerate bought a share of the Willesden Forest Research Centre, he made contact with some rather peculiar people and, to cut a long story short, began running a very unpleasant business inside the Willesden Research Centre. They operated –'

David cried out as if the word suddenly horrified him.

'– I mean they really did operate – sometimes here, sometimes in Australia or Singapore. They had several bases. The medical teams came into the country as tourists, and would wind up at the Willesden Forest Research Centre. Meanwhile, Winnie Finney developed his strange car, and he and Dr Fabrice collected people off the street.'

'When can we get out of hospital?' asked Harley. 'Not that I'm in a hurry,' he added quickly. His big sister had been to see him once, but his father had not been in at all. David thought Harley must be feeling deserted.

'You both seem well recovered from the drug Winnie Finney gave you in the coffee, but they want to keep an eye on you for one more night. We'll collect you both tomorrow,' said David's father. He hesitated, then glanced at his watch. 'Actually Harley, your mother is flying in from Melbourne at this very moment.'

There was a short silence.

'What's she coming for?' Harley muttered at last.

'She was dreadfully upset when she heard about your adventure,' said David's father. 'I know it won't be easy for you, but I think you should try hard – very hard – to be nice to her. And we've arranged for you to stay with us for a few days. I understand your father is having a hard time at work – at least, he's too busy to look after you properly.'

'Ha!' said Harley. 'He's sick of me. He wants a different sort of kid.' David could see he was struggling not to cry. 'I'd like to come, though,' he added quickly. 'And – and it'll be okay, seeing Mum again, I mean.'

'It's because of her you knew about that organ music,' said David. 'And that music was partly what made Winnie Finney see Quinta.'

'Quinta?' asked his father. David and Harley looked at one another and fell silent. The two brain-dead young men had been found in the room off the mortuary, but there had been no sign of any other victims. For some reason Quinta was a secret that could not be talked about – except between themselves.

'David …' Harley said when David's parents had gone, after hugging both boys and promising to collect them as soon as possible. Harley almost never used David's name. Usually he just said, 'Hey you!'

David looked over at him.

'She … she sort of saved our lives twice over, didn't she?' Harley said. 'Quinta, I mean.'

'Suppose so,' said David. 'I think if we'd got into those beds and gone to sleep … well, we wouldn't ever have woken up again. First she stopped Dr Fabrice and then she stopped Winnie Finney.'

'She sure did,' said Harley, shuddering.

'Lucky for us the firemen were true forestry people – nothing to do with any international syndicate,' said David.

'Lucky for us they called the police,' Harley exclaimed, but he was not really thinking about their escape.

'I know all that. But listen! Before Quinta frightened Winnie Finney to death she said she could only be seen because we believed in ghosts, didn't she? She somehow worked through us. And we worked through her. You sort of slung words … like, powerful words … at Winnie Finney and she – she somehow gave the words extra power – ghost power. They hit him like bullets.'

'I don't believe in ghosts,' sighed David. 'I keep on telling you that. Well, I suppose I just might believe in them in a sort of way from now on, but I didn't believe in them last night. I've never believed in them.'

Harley sighed as well. 'I do,' he said simply. 'I always have. I pretended I didn't, because people, you know, my father and sister and other people – you too – always slung off at me.'

David thought about this.

'Well,' he said at last, speaking rather drowsily, 'you believe in ghosts and I read about them. It's part of the same thing, I suppose.'

But Harley did not answer. He had fallen asleep with his hair sticking up like the crest of a startled cockatoo.

And within another minute David had fallen asleep, too, and as he slept, his strong heart beat regularly, and his good lungs breathed smoothly. Every bit of him was working perfectly. And he was so tired that no terrible dreams disturbed his sleeping. He would dream, of course – dream forever – but the dreams would come later.